Eel River Christian Confe~ence

Minutes of the Annual Session of the Eel River Christian Conference

Eel River Christian Conference

Minutes of the Annual Session of the Eel River Christian Conference

ISBN/EAN: 9783337302283

Printed in Europe, USA, Canada, Australia, Japan

Cover: Foto ©Andreas Hilbeck / pixelio.de

More available books at **www.hansebooks.com**

MINUTES

OF THE

Forty-Fourth Annual Session

OF THE

Eel River Christian Conference,

HELD WITH THE

Broadway Christian Church,

NOBLE COUNTY, IND.,

August 17, 18, 19 & 20, 1887.

FORT WAYNE, INDIANA:
D. W. JONES, BOOK & JOB PRINTER, 13 EAST MAIN STREET, 3D. FLOOR.
1887.

OFFICERS OF CONFERENCE.

---◦◦---

President,   JOHN W. SELERS, *Mentone, Ind.*
Vice Prest,   W. MESIMORE, *Sidney, Ind.*
Treasurer,   JOHN P. KITT, *Merriam. Ind.*
Secretary,   PETER WINEBRENNER, *Merriam, Ind.*
Assist. Sec'y,   JOHN P. KITT,   "   "
☞ *All of the above officers were re-elected for the ensuing year.*

---◦---

ROLL OF CHURCHES THAT WILL ENTERTAIN CONFERENCE.

---◦---

1. BLUFFTON, *Wells County*, ...1888.
2. SPARTA, *Noble County* ....1889.
3. XENIA, *Miami County*,............... 1890

---◦---

TRSTEES OF CONFERENCE.
Elected Ang. 1885.

JACOB FRY,...................................... ....*Majenica, Ind.*
W. MESSIMORE, ...*Sidney, Ind.*
ALEXANDER BAYMAN, ...*Piercetou, Ind.*

Elected Aug. 1886.

REYNOLDS WALSER, ...*Bruena Vista, Ind.*
LUTHER W. PULLEN,..............................*Collamer, Ind.*
J. W. WINESBURG,...........................*New Madison, Ind.*

Elected Aug. 1887.

SAMUEL OHLWINE,...............................*Cromwell, Ind.*
A. T. STUDABAKER,...............................*Bluffton, Ind.*
GEORGE McCONNELL,...............................*Sidney, Ind.*

---◦---

EXECUTIVE COMMITTEE.

JOHN W. SELLERS, *President, Mentone, Indiana.*
W. MESSIMORE, *Vice President, Sidney,*   "
JAMES ACHISON, *Piercetou,*   "
DAVID HIDY. *North Manchester,*   "
C. V. STRICKLAND, *Argos,*   "
P. WINEBRENNER, *Sec'y, Merriam,*   "

ORDER OF BUSINESS.

1. Reading of Scriptures, singing and prayer.
2. Appoint two committees: First, on filling the stand for preaching. Second, on fixing the time for meeting and adjourning.
3. Introduction of president-elect, and introductory remarks.
4. Reading of the last half day's minutes of last session.
5. Call the roll of Ministers.
6. Call the roll of Churches.
7. The appointing of committees.
8. Read and consider the minutes of called session (if any) of Conference.
9. Hear the Annual Address.
10. Introduction of visiting brethren.
11. Reports of Ministers
12. Reports of Churches.
13. Reports of Sunday Schools.
14. Reports of Committees.
15. Report of Treasurer; money on hand; his claims, if any.
16. On the publication of the minutes of Conference.
17. Report of the President.
18. Report of the Secretary.
19. Appoint delegates to the State Conference.
20. Appoint delegates to sister conferences.
21. On who shall deliver the annual address.
22. Where shall the next annual session of Conference be held?
23. On providing destitute churches with preaching.
24. Miscellaneous business.

MINUTES.

———o———

FIRST DAY—MORNING SESSION.

The Eel River Christian Conference met in its forty-fourth Annual Session in the Broadway Christian Church, Noble County, Indiana, Wednesday, August 17, 1887, at 10 o'clock, a. m.

The President, J. W. Sellers, called Conference to order. Singing, led by Wm. Knappe. Reading of the Scriptures by Elder Peter Winebrenner, and prayer by Elder J. Rittenhouse.

Singing again by the congregation, after which the President declared Conference open for the transaction of business.

The President appointed T. Whitman, S. Ohlwine and Wm. Knappe a committee to fix the time for meeting and adjournment of Conference; also, to arrange for filling the stand with preaching.

The minutes of the last half-day of last year's session were then read, and stand approved.

ROLL CALL.

Ministers:—G. Abbott, T. Whitman, Wm. S. Manville, Peter Winebrenner, D. McGinnis, D. B. Rollen, Marks, Bolton, Gloyd, Amber and Rittenhouse. Nearly all the ministers came in and reported the first two days.

ROLL OF CHURCHES CALLED.

About twelve Churches responded to this first call. Nearly all responded and reported by 9 o'clock on the third day.

Introduction of Visiting Brethren:—Elds. J. J. Copeland, of Eastern Indiana Conference; J. J. Summerbell, Sec'y of the Quadrennial Convention; Jeannie M. Jones, of Fort Wayne, and Reason Davis, of the Michigan South Western Christian Conference, were introduced and took seats with us.

On motion, a bar was established. G. Abbott and C. V. Strickland were appointed to set the bounds of said bar. From the pulpit to the stoves one side, and center tier of seats at first. This being too small the other side was added to the center seats, and Delegates and Ministers were requested to come within the bar and occupy these seats, which were generally well filled.

On motion, the hour of 2 o'clock was set apart for the Annual Address. When that time arrived, Elder Thomas Whitman, the appointee, came forward, took the stand and delivered the address, which was full of wholesome instruction, and was well delivered.

On motion, a vote of thanks was tendered Elder Whitman for his able address and timely advice.

The committee on filling the stand announced J. J. Copeland for this place, and C. V. Strickland for the Sparta Church, for this evening.

Report on meeting and adjourning:—Meet at 8 o'clock, a. m., and adjourn at 11:30. Meet again at 1:30, p. m., and adjourn at 4, p. m. T. Whitman, S. Ohlwine, Wm. Knappe, committee.

Adjourned, to meet again at 1:30, p. m. Singing by the congregation. Benediction by Elder J. J. Copeland.

————o————

FIRST DAY—AFTERNOON SESSION.

Met at 1,30, as per adjournment. Singing, led by C. V. Strickland. Prayer by J. J. Summerbell. Singing by the congregation. Minutes of the forenoon session read, and approved as read.

REPORTS OF MINISTERS.

ELDER GEORGE ABBOTT, born in 1817; was educated at common school; was converted and joined the church in 1843; entered the ministry in 1846; was ordained at Pleasant Grove Church in '48;

is pastor at Sparta, Smith's School house, and Antioch Churches. Salary promised, $318,00. Amount received, $350,00. Received into church 17; held three protracted meetings; sermons and lectures near 200. Address, North Manchester, Ind.

ELDER JAMES ACHISON, was born in Lewisburg, Ohio, in 1814, was converted and joined church in 1832; entered the ministry in 1837; salary received, $123,00; have done missionary work at Warsaw, Morse School house, and at Claypool; helped others in protracted meetings: sermons. 150. Address, Pierceton, Ind.

ELDER DAVID HIDY. Sermons, 168; members received into church on my charges, 86; in connection with other ministers, 40. Baptized 46; salary promised and paid, $400,00. Held 6 protracted meetings; administered 6 communions. Was pastor at Eel River, Collamer, New Madison and South Coesse. Address, North Manchester, Indiana.

ELDER JACOB RITTINHOUSE:—Was born in Dayton, Ohio, in 1835; entered the ministry in 1863; is pastor of five churches: salary promised, $200,00; amount received, $430,00. Number of persons received into church 12; communions 13. Pastor at North Webster, Purviance Chapel, Chester Center, Warren branch, and one church in Michigan. Address, Wawaka, Noble county, Ind.

ELDER NELSON ABBOTT, was born in Wabash county, Indiana, in 1839; entered the ministry in 1868. Could not preach much on account of throat disease. Can not be with you at Conference. God bless you all. Address, Etna, Indiana.

R. L. AMBER, (licentiate,) was born at Urbana, Wabash county, Ind. Was converted and joined the church in 1876, under Elder Whitman's preaching. Entered the ministry in 1686; is pastor at Sidney, Salamonie, and Pleasant Grove; salary, $60,00; persons received into church 12; in connection with other ministers 60; done misionary work at Salamonie and Pleasant Grove; sermons and addresses 120. Address, Urbana, Indiana.

The Lord has wonderfully blest me in crowning my labors with success during my first year's work. Pray for me.   R. L. A.

Martin Arnold, (licentiate) was born in Maryland, in 1805; age 82 years; was converted and joined the church about 31 years ago, and entered the ministry some sixteen years ago. Address, Claypool, Indiana.

Elder J. W. Bolton, was born in Whitley county, Ind., in 18-49. Entered the ministry in 1885; is pastor at Waterford, Millwood and Leesburg; salary promised $170,00; received $200,00 received into church 11; in connection with other ministers 40. Address, Kinsey, Indiana.

Elder J. H. Gregory, was born in Penn.; aged 79 years; converted and joined church in 1828; entered the ministry in 1852 at Pleasant Grove, Ind. Have preached two funeral discourses, and deliverd some 12 exhortations;—have not done more on account of throat disease. Address, Walkerton, Ind.

Elder D. W. Jones, was born near Dayton, Ohio, in 1821; entered the ministry in 1857; is pastor at Peabody; salary promised $60,00. Have done missionary work at Leesburg, Liberty Center and Fort Wayne. Address, Fort Wayne, Ind.

Elder Wm. B. Jones, was born at Elk Run, Ohio; aged 70 years; converted and joined church in 1840; entered the ministry in 1842. Is in poor health—preaching some; done missionary work at Mill wood; preached some 3 or 4 sermons and several funerals. Address, Millwood. Ind.

Elder Uzal Kimball, was born in Perry county, Ohio, in 1818; joined church in 1842 and entered the ministry in 1850. Took Sugar Grove and the wing of the Warren Church, but was prevented by the sickness of my companion from preaching about 4 months. Sermons 39—done the best I could under the circumstances. My desire for the prosperity of the cause is as strong as ever it was— I will do all that I can in the future. Address, Montpelier, Blackford county, Ind.

Elder W. S. Manville, was born near Sparta, Ohio, in 1819; was educated at common school and college; was converted and joined church in 1840; entered the ministry in 1841; was ordained in '46; is pastor at Antioch Christian Church; salary promised, $100,00; received $102,75. Protracted meetings 1; persons received into church 14; baptized 4; sermons 75. Address, Valparaiso, Indiana.

Elder J. J. MARKLEY. I have preached for the Murray church twice per month during the year, besides a number of funerals. My labor has been without money and without price, yet I am not discouraged. We have a few worthy members, by grace divine I shall stand by them. Remember us in your prayers. We have had prayer meeting nearly every Lord's day, and some very spiritual seasons. Two members have recently departed this life with a bright prospect of that upper and better country. Enclosed is one dollar as Conference fund. May God bless the entire Conference. Address, Murray, Indiana.

Elder V. R. MILLER, was born in Cass county, Mich., in 1841; entered the ministry in 1863; is pastor of Franklin Union and Oak Grove churches, Mich.; salary promised $200,00; received $110,50, will receive the balance at expiration of time—did not commence with beginning of the conference year. Address, Goshen, Ind.

Elder LEVI MARKS, was born in Bedford, Penn., in 1828; entered the ministry in 1870; is pastor at Pleasant Hill and Cottonwood. Salary promised $65'00; received $50,00; persons received into church 2. Address, Pierceton, Indiana.

Elder D. A. McGINNIS, was born in Ohio, 1835; entered the ministry in 1875. Done missionary work all I could. Address, Mount Etna, Huntington county, Ind.

Elder JESSE FANNING, was born in Wayne county, Ind., in 18-20, aged 66 years. Am not well at present,—will not be at the present session of Conference; resided and labored every Sabbath in Kansas up to October. Salary $23,00. Since my return to Indiana have preached but little. May God's blessing rest down upon this session of Conference. Address, North Manchester, Ind.

Elder W. D. SAMUEL, was born in Madison county, Ind., in 18-51; entered the ministry in 1877. Is pastor of churches at Bluff-

ton and Pleasant View.   Salary promised $550,00; received $600,-
00. Persons received into church 27 ; baptized 7.   Done missionary
work half the time in Bluffton.   Address, North Manchester, Ind.

ELDER C. V. STRICKLAND, was born at Easton, Penn., in 1848, is
pastor of the Church at Argos, Plum Tree, Eel River Chapel, and
Shiloe ; salary received from all sources, $527,00.   Persons received
into church 200 ; baptized 87.   My work, excepting the Plum Tree
church, has all been in the North Western Ind. Conference.   Address, Argos, Indiana.

SISTER MARY A. STRICKLAND, was born in Mishawaka, Ind.   Is
pastor at Burroughs, and assistant pastor at Argos, Shiloe, and Eel
River Chapel.   Salary received $509,15 ; persons received into the
Church—assisted in receiving the 200 mentioned in C. V. Strickland's report.   My work has been, principally, as assistant pastor
with my husband, and my labors have been exclusively in the
bounds of the North Western C. Conference.   Address, Argos, Ind.

ELDER P. L. RYKER.—Is pastor at North Manchester, Markle,
and Rock Creek.   Salary promised, $400,00; received $391,00.
Number received into church 33 ; baptized 4. Address, North Manchester, Indiana.

D. B. ROLLEN, (licentiate,) was born in Columbia, Tenn., in 18-
55; entered the ministry in 1881.   Had no church charges.   Assisted in two revival meetings, and received something but kept
no account.   Address, Leesburg, Indiana.

ELDER LOUIS HIMES, was born in Montgomery, Virginia, in 18-
33.   Entered the ministry in 1867.   Amount received not remem-
bered.   Preached 14 sermons, and assisted in a few meetings. Address, Leesburg, Ind.

ELDER THOMAS WHITMAN, was born in Versailles, Ohio, in 1822.
Entered the ministry in 1844; is pastor of church at Broadway.
Salary $88,00; persons received into church 6.   Address, Pierce-
ton, Ind.

ELDER PETER WINEBRENER, was born in Liberty, Ohio, and was
educated at Liberty, and Sanford and Elliott schools, in Indiana.
Converted and joined the Church in 1844 ;entered the ministry in

1857; was ordained at Clear Creek Church in 1859. Is pastor at Merriam, Sugar Grove and Union C. Churches. Salary promised $400,00; received 500,00. Held four protracted meetings—three in my own charges, and one at Broadway, Elder Whitman's charge. Persons received into church about 50, baptized 25. Sermons and lectures 270. Remarks: Health good; a number of the lectures were on the subject of S. D. Adventism. The $100 more salary than promised was donations, also for lectures, marriages and funerals, which makes the amount. Address, Merriam, Noble county, Ind.

GEORGE W. GLOYD, (licentiate,) was born in Ligonier, in 1848; educated at Common School; converted and joined the Church in 1867. Entered the ministry 1886. Sermons and addresses 25. Address, Ligonier, Ind.

ELDER WILLIAM PERDUE, was born in Delaware county, Indiana, in 1832; age 54 years; educated at Common School; converted and joined the Church in 1854; entered the ministry in 1872, and was ordained at Sugar Grove in 1877; is pastor at Kelso, salary $65,00; meetings of days two; received into church 19; baptized 10. Done mission work part of the time. Sermons and addresses 63. Address, Warren, Ind.

ELDER C. C. MORRIS, aged 73 years. No report; is said to be in feeble health. Address, Warren, Ind.

FRANK MOSURE, (licentiate,) born in 1861; entered the ministry in 1882. No report. Address, Vera Cruz, Ind.

RILEY FREEMAN, (licentiate,) was born in Clay county, Kentucky, in 1821; joined the church in 1844, entered the ministry in 1872. No report Address, Urbana, Ind

Ministers Uniting with Conference.—Bro. .J .N. ULLERY, applied for membership in Eel River C. Conference, recommended by the Kelso C. Church.

Sister ELIZA ROBINSON, also applies for membership in Conference, being recommended by the South Coesse Church.

Committee on Reception: J. W. Bolton, C. V. Strickland, D. Hidy.

Both were received into Conference, and the right hand of fellowship extended to them by the ministers.

Report of Ministers Laboring in this Conference, but not members thereof.

ELDER K. E. WEST, was born in Cass county, Indiana, in 1851; entered the ministry in 1877; is pastor at Six Mile and Paw Paw; salary promised $125,00; received $128,00. Persons received into church 24; baptized 17. Address, Bluffton, Indiana. [The above salary must have reference to the Paw Paw Church alone, as he received in all probably, some five or six hundred dollars.—*Sec'y.*

ELDER J. J. COPELAND, entered the ministry in 1880; is pastor at Xenia and Wakarusa; salary $269,00; received into church 75; baptized 18. Address, Xenia, Indiana

ELDER REASON DAVIS, was born in Huron county, Ohio; age 49 years; was converted and joined church in 1871; entered the ministry the same year; was ordained in Kansas in 1883; is pastor at Goshen, Millersburg and Spring Hill; salary promised $475,00; received $290,00. Held 6 protracted meetings, and received into the church 120 members; baptized 34. Held one meeting at Capron, Ill., and one in Pittsford, Mich. Address, Goshen, Indiana.

SISTER JEANNIE M. JONES, (ordained at Markle in 1883) was born in Canada; was educated at Toronto Normal School; am a member of Drayton C. Church, and am licensed by the same to preach. Have not preached more than 100 sermons this year; received 50 persons into church, and baptized 7; was pastor at Clear Creek, and held protracted meetings at Leesburg, Summitville, Greentown & Manchester, outside of my regular work. Severe illness this year necessitated comparative quiet. Address, Fort Wayne, Indiana.

A motion prevailed that, On to-morrow at 10 o'clock, a. m., the Conference will hear ELDER J. J. SUMMERBELL, Sec'y American Christian Quadrennial Convention, present the claims of the same to this Conference.

Adjourned, to meet again to-morrow morning at 8 o'clock. Singing, led by Wm. Knappe; Benediction by Elder Achison.

SECOND DAY—MORNING SESSION

President called Conference to order at 8 o'clock, Singing led by Wm. Knappe; reading of Scripture by J. W. Bolton, Prayer by D. Hidy. Singing again by congregation.

Minutes of yesterday afternoon read and approved. The President then delivered his Address to Conference, which embraced a number of subjects of interest, which were presented with much good sense and forcible reasoning, for which a vote of thanks was tendered him by Conference.

ELDERS REASON DAVIS, of Goshen, and D. S. DAVENPORT, of the Eastern Indiana Conference, were then introduced and invited to seats with us.

REPORTS OF CHURCHES.

ANTIOCH CHURCH: Added by confession 15 , number of members at present 63; baptisms 4; communions 1; pastors' salary $100,00; paid for other preaching $18,00; for mission purposes $3, 45 ; conferdnce fund 1,50. Value of church property $1,500 : Heralds taken 4. The Church was organized in 1862, by Elder G. Abbott. Delegates to conference, J. W. Winesburg & wife, Warren Grub & wife. Pastor, William S. Manville. Address, Valparaiso, Ind.

Andrew Urchel Clerk, North Manchester, Ind.

SABBATH SCHOOL REPORT: Months in the year 6 ; enrolled 57: male scholar 20, females 37; over 15 years of age 23 ; united with the church 25; average attendance 58 ; officers and teachers 9 : S. S. Heralds taken 30 copies; other S. S. papers taken 30. Lesson Leaves, intermediate Bible Class—— Money raised in school 10,00 Andrew Urchel Superintendent, North Manchester, Ind. Emma McCoy Secretary, North Manchester, Ind.

BROADWAY CHURCH: Reported last year 40; added by confession 5; deceased 1; present membership 44; preaching per month 1 ;

pastors' salary $88,00; other preaching $8,00; Children's Mission cause 2,50; educational interests 2,40; Quadrennial 1,70; conference fund 1,50; Conference missionary 6,00. Value of church property $2000,00. Wealth of congregation $20,000,00. Heralds taken 2. Church was organized by Philip Zeigler; delegates, Wm. Knappe, J. N. Ohlwine and D. S. Holverstott. Pastor, T. Whitman, Pierceton, Ind. Samuel Ohlwine Clerk, Cromwell, Ind.

SABBTH SCHOOL: Months in the year 6; enrolled 60; officers and teachers 8; average attendance 40; over 15 years of age 25; united with the church 3; S. S. Heralds and Glad Tidings 50 copies; money raised in school $12,00. Wm. Gerkin Superintendent, Cromwell Ind.

BLUFFTON CHURCH: Added by confession 22; present membership 130; baptized 8; communions 3; Sabbath preaching, per mo., 4 times; prayer meeting once per week; pastor's salary $300,00; other preaching $15,00; contributed for building purposes $425,00; conference fund 2,00. Value of church property $2,500; wealth of congregation $25,000. Heralds of G. L. taken 5. Church was organized in 1883 by W. D. Samuel. Delegates to Conference, Jennie Pence, Alice Ratliff, Sarah Gettle, Cyrus Smith. Pastor, W. D. Samuel, Bluffton, Ind. Churb Clerk, B. F. Straw, Bluffton, Ind.

SABBATH SCHOOL. Months in the year 12; enrolled 100; officers and teachers 14; average attendance 85; pupils above 15 y'rs of age 50; pupils uniting with the church 7; papers—Heralds and Glad Tidings 65 each; money raised about $60. Superintendent S. F. Ratliff, Bluffton. Indiana.

BUENA VISTA CHURCH: Members reported last year 109; added by confession 2; deceased 3; present number 108; communions 1; preaching per month, 2; pastor's salary $130; conference fund 2,10; value of church property $600; Heralds of G. L. taken 3; Church was organized in 1881, by W. D. Samuel. Delegates, R. Walser, H. Morrow, J. Dunbar and G. M Rice. Pastor, D. S. Davenport, Harrisville, Randolph county, Indiana. Lorenzo Dunbar, Church Clerk, Linn Grove, Adams county, Ind.

SABBATH SCHOOL: Months in the year 6; enrolled 45; officers and teachers 12; average attendance 40; over 15 years of age 20; S. S. papers taken—Heralds and Glad Tidings 30 copies each; money raised $9,00. Superintendent, G. M. Rice, Linn Grove, Indiana.

COLLAMER CHURCH: Reported last year 74; added by confession 4; dismissed by letter 3; without letter 3; male members 25; females 47; total present membership 72; preaching per month 3 sermons; prayer meetings per month 4; business meetings 4, or quarterly; baptized 2; communions 1; pastor's salary $100; paid for other preaching $15,00; missionary fund 60 cts., conference fund 1,50; value of church property $1.800; money raised this year $132.00; Heralds of G. L. taken 3; church was organized in 1877; pastor, David Hidy. Delegates, S. Green and wife, Reuben Abbott and wife, John Phillips and wife, and L. W. Pullen and wife. L. W. Pullen Church clerk, Collamer, Indiana.

SABBATH SCHOOL: Months in the year 12; scholars enrolled 65; male scholar 30, females 35; over 15 years of age 25; average attendance 54; officers and teachers 9; S. S. papers taken 40; use Christian Lesson Leaves; money raised $38,00. C. W. Hayden, Superintendent, Eva Smith Secretary, Collamer, Ind.

CLEAR CREEK CHURCH: Reported last year 68; added by confession 13; dismissed by letter 1; without letter 1; present membership 79; baptisms 7; communions 4; preaching per month 1; prayer meetings per week 2; pastor's salary $130; paid mission cause 6,20; for educational purposes 20,00; conference fund 2,00; for local benevolence 3,85; Heralds G. L. taken 4; church was organized in 1850 by G. Abbott. Delegates, G. H. Bailey, John S. Bitner, D. Kaylor and Samuel Gill. Jeannie M. Jones, pastor, Fort Wayne, Ind. Samuel Beck. Church clerk, Huntington, Ind.

SABBATH SCHOOL; Months in the year 12; enrolled 65; officers and teachers 10; average attendance 45; above 15 years of age 20; united with the church 8; papers taken—Sunday School Herald and Glad Tidings. Money raised in the school $20. Superintendent, G. H. Bailey, Miss Ellie Beck Secretary, Huntington, Ind.

SOUTH COESSE CHURCH : Reported last year 77 ; added by confesion 23 ; dismissed by letter 3 ; dismissed without letter 23 ; deceased 2 ; present membership 72 ; communions 2 ; preaching per month 1 ; prayer meeting once per week. Pastor's salary $111,75 Paid for other preaching 5,30 ; for missions cause 3,15 ; for educational purposes 12,00 ; value of church property $1000. Conference fund 2,00 ; Heralds taken 2 ; Church was organized in 1854. Delegates, Eliza Robinson, George Whicker & wife ; pastor, David Hidy, North Manchester, Ind. Albert Bush clerk, Coesse, Ind.

COESSE SABBATH SCHOOL : Months in the year 6 ; enrolled 49 ; officers and teachers 8 ; average attendance 30 ; united with the church 12 ; S. S. Heralds 25 ; money raised 9,24. Superintendent Albert Bush ; Secretary, George York, Coesse, Ind.

CHRUBUSCO C. CHURCH : Not reported. A committee was appointed to visit them.

EEL RIVER CHURCH : Reported last year 100 ; added by confession 21 ; dismissed without letter 2 ; deceased 2 ; present membership 119 ; baptized 11 ; communions 1 ; prayer meetings per week 1 ; pastor's salary $100 ; paid for other preaching 7,25 ; contributed to mission cause 2,50 ; conference fund 1,50. Value of church property $1000 ; Heralds of G. L. taken 6. Church was organized 1840 ; delegates, John Smith, Aaron M. Simpson, Brother Shoaf & wife, Brother Walgamuth & wife. Pastor, David Hidy, North Manchster, Ind. Wm. Brubaker Church clerk, South Whitley, Ind.

SABBATH SCHOOL : Months in the year 12 ; enrolled 90 ; officers and teachers 13 ; average attendance 79 ; over 15 years of age 55 ; united with the church 10 ; money raised in school 11,10. Superintendent, James Circle, Secretary, Dora Miles

GOSHEN C. CHURCH : Reported last year 47 ; added by confession 3 ; present membership 50 ; communions 3 ; preaching per month 4 times ; prayer meetings per week, one ; pastor's salary $115,00 ; paid children's mission 3,45 ; conference fund 2,15 ; value of church property $2,500. Heralds of Gospel Liberty taken 20 ; Church was organized in 1886, by Elder Reason Davis. Delegates,

Elders Reason Davis and V. R. Miller. Pastor, R. Davis, Goshen, Ind. Ellen Ulery Church clerk, Goshen, Ind.

GOSHEN SABBATH SCHOOL: Was organized June 27, 1886; number of months organized 14; during the year 12; average attendance 55; money raised in the School $31,87; Children's Easter collection 3,03; use the Christian literature, published Dayton, O. Superintendent, Sol Ulery; Secretary, Eliza R. Miller, Goshen, Ind. Remarks: Our School has maintained a good interest during the time. Our Children's Day was a success—raised 3,45. Niona Bailey, a little Miss scarcely five years old, gave an Ice-cream social to a party of her little friends, and raised 60 cents, which she turned over to the Sunday School, an example worthy of imitation by many older persons. E. Miller, Secretary.

KELSO C. CHURCH: Reported last year 88; added by confession 18; by letter 1; deceased 1; present membership 106; baptized 4; communions 1; preaching per month twice; prayer meetings per week 1; pastor's salary $65,00; paid for other preaching $28,00; paid for building purposes $28,50; conference fund 1,60; value of Church property $1000; wealth of congregation $60,000; Heralds taken 1. Wm. Perdue pastor, Warren, Ind. Delegates, Bro. & Sister Craig, Bro. & Sister Ulery, Bro. & Sister Cassidy. Miller Morgan Church clerk, Majenica, Ind.

KELSO SABBTH SCHOOL: Months in the year 12; enrolled 80; officers and teachers 10; average attendance 40; over 15 years of age 25; united with the Church 5; papers taken—S. S. Heralds and Glad Tidings 30 copies each, quarterlies 40, and 40 intermediate; 15 Little Teachers. Money raised $12,20. Superintendent, J. Ulery, Majenica, Ind. Our School is in a flourishing condition.

LEESBURG CHURCH: Reported last year 43; added by confession 5; deceased 1; present membership 47; communions 1; Sabbath preaching per month 2 times; pastor's salary promised for 6 months $60,00; paid for other preaching $23,10; conference fund 4,75; value of church property $3000; Heralds taken 4; Church was organized in 1869, by George Abbott and D. W. Fowler. Delegates, John Dorsey, Wm. Clay, Mrs. Jennie Rollen and Miss

Jennie Sanderson. J. W. Bolton pastor, Kinzie, Ind. Joseph A. Lay, Church clerk, Leesburg, Ind.

LEESBURG S. SCHOOL: Months in the year 6; enrolled 69; officers and teachers 14; average atten dance 59; over 15 years of age 43; united with the Church 1; money raised in school 7,04. Superintendent, Mrs. Baugher, Secretary, Jennie Sanderson, Leesburg, Ind.

MILLWOOD CHURCH: Reported last year 73; added by confession 5; by letter 1; present membership 79; communions 2; Sabbath preaching per month 1; pastors salary $60,00; other preaching $60,00; paid mission cause 1,00; conference fund 2,00; value of church property $800,00; wealth of congregation $40,000; Heralds taken 2; Church was organized in 1856 by Elder G. Abbott. Delegates, Wm. Jones and wife, George Snively and wife, Jacob Whiteleather and wife, P. H. Bowman and wife, and V. Hammon. Pastor, J. W. Bolton, Kinzie, Ind. Wm. B. Anglin, Church clerk, Etna Green, Ind.

MILLWOOD S. SCHOOL: Months in the year 6; enrolled 75; officers and teachers 16; average attendance 60; over 15 years of age 40; money raised in school 6,14. Superintendent, Wm. B. Anglin, Etna Green, Ind.

MARKLE C. CHURCH; Reported last year 56; added by confession 1; by letter 2; dismissed by letter 1; without letter 1; deceased 2; present number 55. Communions 2, preaching once per month; pastor's salary $82,00; conference fund 3,00. Heralds taken 1. Church was organized in 1876, by Elder D. W. Fowler. Delegates, George Watson, D. Stockman, H. L. Hoover. Pastor, P. L. Ryker, North Manchester, Ind. Wm. Keller, Church clerk, Markle, Ind.

MARKLE SABBATH SCHOOL: Our S. School is a Union School— made up of different denominations: Superintendent, James Ratcliff, Markle, Ind.

MERRIAM C. CHURCH: Reported last year 150; added by confession 5, by letter 2; deceased 3; members at present time 1,54. Baptised 9: communions 1; preaching per month 2. Pastor's salary, $144,00, (more promised, will be paid.) Paid for other preaching $37,00. Paid for building purposes $25,00. Contributed to Children's Mission Fund 3,60. Conference fund 5,00 ; Conference Mission 6,30. Value of Church property $4000. Wealth of congregation $75000. Heralds taken 12. Other religous papers taken 1. Church was organized in 1843, by Rev. Peter Banta. Delegates, J. R. Young and wife, J. Kepford and wife, Sisters Boyer, Marker, and Winebrenner, and J. McMeans. Pastor, Peter Winebrenner. John P. Kitt, Church clerk, Merriam, Ind.

MERRIAM SABBATH SCHOOL: Months in the year 12. Enrolled 96, officers and teachers 12, average attendance 64, over 15 years of age 45, united with the Church 3, papers taken—S. S. Heralds. Glad Tidings and Little Teacher, 115, vol. 100. Money raised in School $56,71. Superintendent, J. P. Kitt. C. W. Kitt, Secretary.

MURRAY CHURCH: Brief report by J. J. Markley; they have some 30 members; Markley is preaching for them; they are keeping up prayer meeting and hope to be able to live. God grant it.—Sec'y.

NEW MADISON CHURCH: Reported last year 94; added by confession 35; by letter 1; moved away 3; present membership 130; baptisms 12; Sabbath preaching per month 1; prayer meetings per week from 1 to 2: pastor's salary $88,00; paid for other preaching $22,50, paid to local mission cause 5,25; conference fund 4,15; value of church property $1,500; Heralds taken 6: church was organized in 1849 by Rev. James Atchison; delegates, R. Shawbut, G. Elliott and wife, U. Shook and wife; pastor, D. Hidy, N. Manchester, Ind., J. N. Foust Secretary, Servia, Ind.

SABBATH SCHOOL: Months in the year 12; scholars enrolled 60; male scholars 20, female 40; over 15 years of age 20; have united with the church 12; average attendance 65; officers and teachers 16; S. S. Heralds taken 55; other S. S. papers taken 55: used Berean quarterlies and intermediate lesson leaves 5 copies: money raised in school $26.00. George W Elliott superintendent, Ollie Krisher Secretary, Servia, Ind. Remarks: Our school is in a prosperous condition, and we hope through it to accomplish a good work for the Master Jesus.

NORTH MANCHESTER CHURCH: Number reported last year 51; added by confession 18; by letter 2; deceased 1; members at present time 70; baptisms 1; communions 2; preaching per month 2; prayer meeting per week 1, a part of the time; pastor's salary $200; paid for other preaching about 50.00; contributed for local missionary cause 1.40; conference fund 1.25; value of church property $3,500; wealth of congregation $50,000. Heralds taken 8; church was organized in 1884 by James Atchison, G. Abbott, D. Hidy and P. Winebrenner; delegates L. Smith, G. Kitterman and wife; Pastor P. L. Ryker; church clerk Phillip Shaffer, N. Manchester, Ind.

SABBATH SCHOOL: Months in the year 12; enrolled 78; officers and teachers 9; average attendance 41; use our own literature published at Dayton, O.; money raised in school $13.03; Superintendent Sister Blackwell, North Manchester, Ind.

OAK HILL CHURCH. No report for several years. [I visited them after conference session. They will make an effort to live.] Sec'y.

PLUM TREE CHURCH: Reported last year 166; added by confession 3; dismissed by letter 4; without letter 8; members at present time 154; baptisms 3; communions 3; preaching per month 1; prayer meetings weekly; pastor's salary $125: paid for missionary cause 5:00; contributed to educational interests $100; conference fund 2.00; value of church property $800; wealth of congregation $25,000. Heralds taken 3; church was organized in 1846; delegates F. Fry, M. M. Sowers. Pastor C. V. Strickland, Argos, Ind., E. B. Sparks church clerk, Plum Tree Ind.

SABBATH SCHOOL: Months in the year 12; enrolled 100; officers and teachers 16; average attendance 65; united with the church 3. Literature quarterlies and Tittle Leacher 100; money raised in school $12.00. Superintendent B. Devore.

PAW PAW CHURCH: Reported last year 82; added by con

fession 23; by letter 1; dismissed by letter 3; members at present time 103; baptisms 17; communions 1; preaching per month 1; prayer meeting per week 1; pastor's salary $125; contributed for building purposes $80; conference fund 2.00; value of church property $500; wealth of congregation $40,000; Heralds taken 3; church was organized in 1848 by J. Spenser; delegates, S. Long and Joseph Amber. Pastor K. E West, Bluffton, Ind., Alexander Freman Church clerk, Urbana, Ind.

SABBATH SCHOOL: Months in the year 6; enrolled 94; officers and teachers 14; average attendance 78; above 15 years of age 35; united with the church 16; use Christian quarterlies and Little Teacher published at Dayton, Ohio. Money raised in school 9.00. Superintendent Joseph Amber, Urbana, Ind.

PEABODY CHURCH: Reported last year 47; dismissed without letter 13; present membership 34; communions 2; preaching per month 1; prayer meetings per week 1; pastor's salary $32.85; conference fund 1.75. Church was organized in 1885 by Jeannie Jones; delegates, Daniel Johnson, W. Shrader; pastor D. W. Jones, Fort Wayne, Ind., Joseph Neller church clerk, Columbia City, Ind.

SABBATH SCHOOL: Months in the year 4; enrolled 40; officers and teachers 8; average attendance 30; above 15 years of age 12; S. S. Heralds 20 copies; money raised in four months 5.50; Superintendent Ruth Shearer.

PLEASENT VIEW CHURCH: Reported 95; added by confession 5; members at the present time 100; communions 3; preaching per month 2; prayer meetings per week 1; pastor's salary $100; contributed for missionary cause 3.00; value of church property $2,000; aggregated wealth of congregation $25,000; Heralds taken 1; church was organized in 1885 by W. D. Samuel. Delegate, Daniel Glass; pastor W. D. Samuel, North Manchester, Ind. Jonathan Bender secretary, Bluffton, Ind.

SABBATH SCHOOL: Months in the year 6; enrolled 125; officers and teachers 12; average attendance 80; over 15 years of age 50;

S. S. papers 40 copies; money raised in the school $20.   Superintendent Jonathan Bender, Bluffton, Ind.

PLEASANT GROVE CHURCH: Reported last year 42; added by confession 3; dismissed by letter 2; members at present time 42; preaching per month 1; prayer meetings 1 per week for three months; contributed to pastor's salary $34; paid for other preaching $12.38.   Conference fund 2.50; church was organized in 1845 by Joseph Roberts. Delegates, F. Bowen, Mary Feagler, M. Snideman.   Pastor R. L. Amber, Urbana, Ind., Frank Bowen Church clerk, Liberty Mills, Ind.

SABBATH SCHOOL: Months in the year 4; enrolled 90; officers and teachers 14; average attendance 67; above 15 years of age 32; have united with the church 3; S. S. Heralds 40 copies; money raised in school $15.56. Superintendent Frank Bowen; Edith Clevenger secretary, North Manchester, Ind.

PLEASANT HILL CHURCH: Reported last year 22, added by confession 2; deceased 1; members at present time 23; communions 2; Sabbath preaching per month 1; pastor's salary $40; conference fund 2.00; value of church property $300; wealth of congregation $1,500; church was organized in 1846 by Rev. James Atchison; delegates, T. S. Butt and J. F. Tincheon; pastor Elder Marks, Pierceton, Ind., J. H. Swigert Church Clerk, Wawaka, Ind.

SABBATH SCHOOL: Months in the year 7; enrolled 26; officers and teachers 6; average attendance 15; over 15 years of age 6; money raised in school 2.27. Superintendent N. B. Hathaway.

PLEASANT HILL (near Warren): No report. Last year reported a membership of 44. It also reported a Sabbath school average attendance 65. J. M. Griffith, Secretary, Warren, Ind.

PURVIANCE CHAPEL: Reported last year 48; added by confession 2: added by letter 1; dismissed by letter 1; deceased 1; present membership 50; communions 4; preaching per month 1; paid pastor $60; conference fund 2.00; value of church property $1,000; Heralds taken 4; church was organized in 1870 by

Zeigler and Hidy   Pastor J. Rittinhouse, J. H. Purviance church clerk, Rivers, Ind.

NORTH WEBSTER CHURCH: Reported last year 45; added by confession 1; dismissed 1; deceased 1; present membership 44; communions 3; preaching per month 1; pastor's salary $72; contributed for missionary cause 4.40; conference fund 2.00. Heralds taken 2; church was organized in 1882 by Elder James Atchison. Delegates, I. Witmer, Silas Huber, D. Garber and David Mock. Pastor Rev. Jacob Rittinhouse, Wawaka, Ind., Silas Huber Church clerk, North Webster, Kosciusko Co., Ind.

SABBATH SCHOOL: Months in the year 6; enrolled 70; officers and teachers 10; average attendance 60; over 15 years of age 35; united with the church 12; S. S. Heralds taken; money raised in the school 7.44. Superintendent, James Mock, N. Webster, Ind.

ROCK CREEK, (changed to LIBERTY UNION) CHURCH, reported last year 64; added by confession 12; dismissed by letter 1; present membership 74; baptisms 3; communions 2; Sabbath preaching per month 1; prayer meetings weekly most of the time. Pastor's salary $97; conference funds 1.50; paid Quadrennial 1.00. The church is a union house. Heralds taken 1. Pastor, P. L. Ryker, North Manchester; Ind., H. Dalrymple Church clerk; address, Liberty Center, Wells Co. Ind. The Sabbath school is a union school.

SPRING HILL CHURCH: This church has been reorganized by Elder R. Davis, March 25, 1887 and prays to become or be continued a member of Eel River Christian Conference. We organized with 15 members; added since 32; dropped one; baptisms 17; present membership 46. Sabbath preaching twice a month; prayer meeting weekly; paid pastor $100. Easter collection 2.40. Children's collection 2.03; conference fund 1.50. Rev. R. Davis pastor, Goshen, Ind. Delegates to conference, Francis Ott and wife, John Grimes and wife, Elizabeth Growcock. Church clerk, James Growcock, Ligonier, Ind.

This Church sent up a lengthy address, covenant, and both the new and old organizations, which are too lengthy for record in the minutes, also a recommend of Rev. R. Davis, that he receive a recommend from this conference. (The Goshen church gave R· Davis a recommend for the same purpose,) which request was granted and the desired recommend given R. Davis. *Sec'y.*

SABBATH SCHOOL: Months in the year 6; enrolled 60; officers and teachers 12; average attendance 45; united with the church 11; S. S. Heralds taken 35; other S. S. papers taken 35; money raised $7.69; Bible class quarterlies used. James Growcock Superintendent, Secretary Miss M. Billman. Remarks: I am happy to say that at present the Sabbath school is in splendid condition. J. G.

SIX MILE CHURCH: Reported last year 156, deceased 1, present membership 155; pastor's salary $250. Church clerk, Jonathan Mosure, Vera Cruz, Ind. Pastor K. E. West, Bluffton, Ind· Reported by W. D. Samuel. Secretary John Mosure, Bluffton.

SABBATH SCHOOL: Months in the year 9; enrolled 85; average attendance 69¾; officers and teachers 16. S. S. Heralds and Little Teacher 40 copies each. Volumns in library 200. Christian literature used; money raised $9,54. O. P. Markley, superintendent, Allen Thomas secretary. Address of both Bluffton, Ind.

SIDNEY CHURCH: Total membership 47; communions 1; baptisms 18; preaching once per month. Paid pastor $25; value of church property $1,200. Church was organized in 1886. Delegates, George McConnell, W. Messimore. Messimore, Secretary.

SABBATH SCHOOL: Number of months in the year 12; enrolled 92; average attendance 60; officers and teachers 16; money raised $27.39. A. E. Musselman, Secretary, Sidney, Ind.

SMITH'S SCHOOL HOUSE CHURCH: The above named church was changed from Smith's School house to the Chrisrian Church of Thorn Creek Township, Whitley county. Reported last year 45; added 6. Present membership 51. Sabbath preaching per month 1. Pastor's salary $74.31, paid for other preaching $16. Contributed for building purposes $600 ; for missionary cause, home mission 4.65 ; conference fund 1.69; probable value of church house $700.00. Wealth of congregation $9,000.00; Heralds taken 1; Church was organized in 1868 by Rev. A. Burkett; delegates Howard Simmons, George Grabill, Jacob Scott and Mrs. Scott. Pastor, Rev. George Abbott; Jacob Fisher Church clerk, Columbia City, Ind.

SABBATH SCHOOL: Months in the year 6; enrolled 43; officers and teachers 7; average attendance 56; above fifteen years of age 16; united with the church 3; money raised in school 3.14. Z. W. Grabill, Superintendent.

SPARTA CHURCH: Reported last year 47; added by confession 7; total present membership 54; preaching per month 1; prayer meeting weekly. Fellowship and business meetings 1; communions 1; pastor's salary $125.00; paid for other preaching $20.80. conference fund 2.00. Value of church property $2,500.00. Total money raised $169.50. Heralds taken 2. Church was organized Dec. 15, 1875. Pastor G. Abbott; delegates, Mrs. Jane Whirlege. Walter Wolf. Wm. K. Wolf Church clerk, Ligonier, Ind.

SABBATH SCHOOL: Months in the year 6; enrolled 130; officers and teachers 16; average attendance 65; S. S papers 120; money received $16.83; use Comprehensive Lesson quarterlies. W. Doll superintendent, Myra White secretary, address Ligonier, Ind.

SUGAR GROVE CHURCH: Reported last year 18; added by confession 2; present membership 20; baptisms 3; communions 1; preaching per month one trip 3 sermons each trip. Pastor's salary $102; paid for other preaching $2.25; contributed to children's missionary cause $3.35, home mission 2.60. Conference fund $2.29; value of church property $1,000. Heralds taken 4, other religious papers 2; church was organized in 1850 by Revs. George Abbott and George Patten. Delegates, E. Myers and wife, R. Judy, C. Collett and N. Kyler. Pastor, Peter Winebrenner, Merriam, Ind., Cnurch clerk, Millie Kyler, Liberty Mills. Ind.

SABBATH SCHOOL: Months in the year 6; enrolled 26; officers and teachers 8; average attendance 24; above fifteen years of age 12; use Weekly Magnet 20 copies; money raised in school 3.32. Superintendent B. H. Humbarger, Collamer, Ind., secretary Nannie Kyler, Liberty Mills, Ind.

SALIMONIE CHURCH: Number of members 35; preaching per month 1; paid pastor $10; conference fund 50 cents; value of church property $450. Heralds taken 2, other religious paper 1; church was organized in 1859 by G. Abbott. Delegate, Laura McGinnis. Pastor, Robert Amber; D. A. McGinnis Church clerk, Mt. Etna, Ind.

SABBATH SCHOOL: Enrolled 60; officers and teachers 9; average attendance 46; above 15 years of age 25; papers taken—our own. Money raised in school $5. Superintendent J. E. Jennings.

UNION CHRISTIAN CHURCH: Reported last year 124; added by confession 17; deceased 1. Some of our members joined at Sidney, helped to make up that church. Others have moved away, reducing our membership to 95. Baptisms 7; communions 1; Sabbath preaching per month one trip, three sermons each trip. Pastor's salary $100; paid for other preaching $3; contributed for incidental purposes 1.89; contributed for conference 3.68; contributed for educational interests 2.00; for Quadrennial expenses 1.39; annual conference fund 2.13; for home mission 2.60; value of church property $1.500; Heralds 4; church was organized in 1845 by James Atchison. Delegates, J. N. Compton and wife, J. Bayman and wife, H. W. McConnel and wife. Pastor, P. Winebrenner, Merriam, Ind., Lewis Bayman Church clerk, Collamer, Whitley Co., Ind.

SABBATH SCHOOL: Months in the year 7; enrolled 77; officers and teachers 14; average attendance 60; above 15 years of age 52; united with the church 6; money raised in the school 2.96. Superintendent Lewis Bayman, Collamer, Ind.

WATERFORD CHURCH: Reported last year 56; added by confession 1; dismissed by letter 2; without letter 2; deceased 3;

present membership 48; baptisms 1; communions 2; preaching per month one visit. Pastor's salary $50; contributed for building purposes $68; for missionary cause 1.60; annual conference fund 1.69; local benevolence 50 cents. Value of church property $800; Heralds of Gospel Liberty taken 5; church was organized in 1862 by Elder Peter Banta. Delegates, H. Holsinger, Mrs. L. A. Richards, P. L. West and Mr. and Mrs. Howel. Pastor J. W. Bolton, Kinzie, Ind., Maria M. Miser,er Church clerk, Goshen, Ind.

SABBATH SCHOOL: Months in the year 9; number of pupils enrolled 55; officers and teachers 14; average attendance 37; use Christian lesson leaves; money raised in the school $6.67. Superintendent George S. Castetter.

WAKARUSA CHURCH: Members reported last year 53; added by confession 4; dismissed by letter 1; without letter 2; deceased 2; members at present 52; baptisms 1; communions 2. Sabbath preaching per month twice half of the time; prayer meetings weekly. Pastor's salary $125; paid missionary cause 1.50; conference fund 1.50. Value of church property $1,000; aggregate wealth of congregation $25,000. Heralds taken 7; church was organized by G. Abbott and P. Winebrenner. Delegates, A. Lockwood, D. R. Longenecker and Sister Weintz. Alternates Dr. Knepple, D. V. Werntz and Sister Wire. J. J. Copeland pastor, Xenia, Ind., D. V. Wertz Church clerk, Wakarusa, Ind.

SABBATH SCHOOL: Months in the year 12; pupils enrolled 60; officers and teachers 17; average attendance 40; above 15 years of age 30; united with the church 1. Use Christian quarterlies and Little Teacher, 25 each; money raised in the school 9.81. Superintendent D. C. Grove, Wakarusa, Ind.

WARREN CHURCH: Reported last year 296; added 63; dismissed by letter 2; deceased 3; members at present time 354; baptisms 3; Sabbath preaching per month, twice, a part of the time. Prayer meetings per week once. Pastor's salary $135; paid for other preaching $15; conference fund 2.00; value of church property

$3,500; Herald of Gospel Liberty taken, about 10.   Pastor, J. L. Puckett, Kokomo, Ind , Wm. Hubbard Church clerk, Warren, Ind.

SABBATH SCHOOL: Months in the year 12: pupils enrolled 159; officers and teachers 20; average attendance 96; united with the church 11; use Christian leaves and Little Teacher; money raised in school $26.75.   Superintendent, John Shaw.

XENIA CHURCH: Reported last year 27; added by confession 55; dismissed without letter 1; deceased 3; members at present time 78; baptisms 17; communions 1; prayer meetings per week 1; pastor's salary $108.24; paid for other preaching $10; for building purposes $700; conference fund 1.90;   value of church property $1,000; wealth of congregation $20,000; Heralds taken 2; church was organized in 1886 by Rev. J. J. Copeland.   Delegates C. G. Babcock and J. J. Copeland.   Pastor, J. J. Copeland, Xenia, Ind , Nathan Johnson Church clerk, Xenia, Ind.

SABBATH SCHOOL: Months in the year 12; enrolled 125; officers and teachers 16; enrolled 70; over 15 years of age 50; united with the church 12; take Glad Tidings and S. S. Heralds 100 copies;   money raised in school $25.   Superintendent C. G. Babcock, Xenia, Ind.

TRAVISVILLE UNION SCHOOL: Months in the year 6; enrolled 60; officers and teachers 12: average attendance 47; use Christian quarterlies; money raised in school 4.25.   Cyrus F. Smith Superintendent, Dela Feals Secretary, Bluffton, Ind.

SALIMONY UNION SABBATH SCHOOL: Was organized April 24, 1887; average attendance of pupils 29;   average officers and teachers 4¾, of visitors 12; average attendance 45¾;   money raised in school 5.01 and was paid out as follows: For lesson leaves 2.43, cards 89 cents, hymn books 75 cents, primmers 29 cents.   Total expenditure $4,16.   Used Christian lesson leaves.   The school is flourishing.   Superintendent J. E. Jennings; Assistant Mrs. G. W. Gundy; Secretary Flo. Weller.

Churches Uniting with Conference at this Session.

Committee on reception of members report. The Christian church at Sidney, Kosciusko Co., Ind., comes to us desiring membership. We recommend their reception. Their report is recorded among the church reports. They were received. J. W. Bolton, C. V. Strickland and D. Hidy, Committee.

Also the Christian church at Millersburg comes to us desiring membership. We also recommend that they be received. The report was adopted. Bolton, Strickland, Hidy, Com.

Their report is as follows: We the Christian church at Millersburg, Elkhart Co., Ind., was organized Dec. 16, 1886, by Elder Reason Davis. We desire admission into the Eel River Christian Conference. Number of charter members 16; present membership 53. We have officers as follows: One ruling Elder, two Deacons and one Church Clerk. We also contribute 2.00 to the conference fund. Delegates to conference, Andie Wetherell and wife, John Kunklin and wife, N. C. Woodcock and wife; Ida Woodcock Church clerk.

Some letters from the Secretary of the North Manchester Christian Church relative to illegal proceedings against an aged member of the church and conference, was read and by motion was referred to the committee on aggrievances.

Time, 10 A. M., voted to J. J. Summerbell for remarks on the Quadrennial, came, when J. J. S. came forward and spoke in high, hopeful and glowing terms of the Christians, their work and bright prospects for the future.

Adjourned until 1:30 p. m. Singing led by Wm. Knappe. Benediction by Rev. D. S. Davenport.

SECOND DAY—AFTERNOON SESSION.

Met per adjournment, 1:30 o'clock. Singing as usual before and after prayer. Prayer by Elder Marks.

Minutes of the forenoon session was read and stand approved.

The J. J. Summerbell Resolutions.

Resolved. That this Conference directs the Secretary to use the blanks which shall be adopted by the American Christian Convention for Conference, Church, Sabbath school reports and others, without further authority from conference, when such blanks shall have been adopted and published by the committee appointed by the convention for that purpose.

2d. Resolved. That this conference recommend to all the churches and ministers to respond to the calls of the American Christian Convention, through its secretary, for the following collections annually: For the Convention on Christmas; for education on Easter Sunday; for Home Mission on Children's Day, the second Sunday in June; and for Foreign Missions the first Sunday in October.

3d. Resolved. That this conference recommend to the churches to use the blanks furnished them by the secretary of the convention in making reports to the Secretary of Conference and to the Treasury of the Convention, of the sum taken up in the annual collections for general purposes, and for forwarding such sums to the Treasurer of the Convention.

4th. Resolved. That the ministers residing within the bounds of this conference, who are not members of this conference, be requested to conform to the general regulations and recommendations of the conference, the same as members, wherever such requirements do not conflict with their duties to the conference of which they are enrolled members; and

Resolved. That we recommend to our churches to employ only such pastors as will accept and abide by the spirit of their resolutions.

5th. Resolved. That the church clerks be requested to state in the report to conference the number of members of the church who contribute regularly to the support of the Gospel; (this contribution not to be construed as referring to an occasional gift in the collection basket, but only to gifts, whether in collection baskets or not, that are regular and stated.)

6th. *Resolved*, that the ministers and churches be requested to consent to the adoption and carrying out of the following resolutions until such time as the brethren may, in conference, amend them, or abolish them:—

7th. *Resolved*, that the Secretary of conference be directed to arrange with ministers who have no regular charges as pastors, and with churches that are destitute of preaching, as far as possible and not objected to by ministers and churches, in the following manner:—

The ministers who are not pastors, and are not superannuated, shall go once a month, or once in two months, or once in three months, according to the direction of the Secretary of conference, to such church and on such a Sunday to hold service there as the conference officer shall appoint.

The churches shall receive ministers sent to them thus, and pay them such sum of money as may be raised in the following manner:—

Cards of the accompanying form shall be circulated in the congregation, by the proper church officer. The church officer is requested to distribute these cards, and afterward to distribute envelopes to the persons who make answer by the cards; and on the visit of the minister the sums received in the envelopes, which should be placed in the collection basket, which should be passed at each preaching service, are to be paid to the visiting minister. This sum shall constitute his compensation, and he shall not ask from the church or conference any further payment; but shall report at the next session of conference, to the conference, in such manner as the conference shall determine, the sums received from these churches, and his opinion and judgement as to whether the churches have done their duty according to their financial ability.

If any church secures its own preaching it is not requested to enter into this arrangement, and any minister, who becomes for any church a regular preacher, is not expected to take part in this arrangement; that is, all churches and ministers who attend to preaching and the support of the gospel, respectivly for themselves, are not expected to take part in this arrangement.

The conference secretary shall send the ministers to the churches in rotation one after the other; that is, he shall so arrange that the same minister does not go for two trips successively to the same church, unless the church make special request, sufficiently long beforehand to enable the conference secretary to arrange the other appointments conveniently, and the compensation is arranged between the minister and the church accordingly; then such minister and church shall be dropped from the list of those engaged in this co-operative work.

When any church ceases to provide for itself, however, as soon as the conference secretary learns that fact, it shall be his duty to include that church in the list for co-operation with the other destitute churches; as soon as it is definitely determined that the church is neglecting to supply its own pulpit, or unable to do so.

8th. *Resolved*, that the conference secretary be allowed the sum of $20 for postage and stationary; and if it be advisable to print blanks for his use in giving notices to the churches and ministers, that he shall advise with the Secretary of the American Christian Convention, and use the blanks that are used elsewhere for this purpose, and that the expense of printing or buying such blanks be paid out of the treasury of conference.

9th. *Resolved*, that it shall be considered the duty of the various ministers who visit the churches under this arrangement of the conference to pursue that course of conduct that shall operate for the upbuilding of the cause locally, and for bringing the church into close connection with the conference, and for stimulating the church to take care of its own affairs as far as is practicable; especially remembering that this arrangement is not designed to assist those churches that can and do carry on their own affairs successfully, but only those which neglect, or are unable, to sustain preaching.

10th. *Resolved*, that the secretary be paid out of the conference treasury for the sums expended by him in carrying out the provisions for the supply of destitute churches.

11*th. Resolved*, that the secretary of Conference be directed annually to visit, either upon a week day or Sunday, each church of the conference that is without a regular pastor, to ascertain the cause of such destitution, and to put into operation the plans adopted by the conference.

All of the above resolutions were presented, read and moved by J. J. Summerbell. They were presented and voted upon one at a time. Each and all prevailed.

Committees Appointed by the President.

1 *Ordination*, James Atchison, Wm. Manville and Peter Winebrenner.

2 *Finance*, C. V. Strickland, Wm. Perdue and J. P. Kitt.

3 *Sabbath School*, Jeannie Jones, George Gloyd and D. A. McGinnis.

4 *Temperance*, Mary A. Strickland, Jeannie Jones and George Whicker.

5 *Christian Union*, David Hidy, Benjamin Benner and R. L. Amber

6 *Publications*, D. W. Jones, D. Hidy and C. V. Strickland.

7 *Education*, Wm. Manville, Jeannie Jones and Wm. Perdue.

8 *Reception of Members*, J. W. Bolton, D. Hidy and C. V. Strickland.

9 *Woman's Rights*, P. L. Ryker, Jeannie Jones and E. Roberts.

10 *Relation of Church to Conference*, C. V. Strickland, D. W. Jones and L. Himes.

11 *Advisability of Pastorates*, George Abbott, W. D. Samuel and J. J. Copeland.

12 *Advisability of placing a man in the field*. W. D. Samuel, W. Messimore and V. R. Miller.

13 *Advice to the Ministry*, L. Compton Levi Smith and Alex. Bayman.

14 *Advice to the Laity*, James Atchison, Levi Marks and V. R. Miller.

15 *Aggrievances*, Thomas Whitman, C. V. Strickland and

Samuel Ohlwines.

16 *Mission, or more paying churches*, Jeannie Jones, Wm. Manville and W. Messimore.

A motion prevailed that the credentials of Brother Frank Mosure be withheld until we have some kind of a report from him.

It was moved that the secretary of the conference give Elder Reason Davis a recommend to his own conference, he having labored almost continuously in the bounds of this conference. Prevailed.

A motion prevailed that the Leesburg C. church be required to pay the principal only on the amount due conference, if paid by the 12th day of December next.

An intermission of five minutes was granted, then after singing, business was resumed.

A motion prevailed that a committee be appointed to look after the Churubusco church, and if necessary to unite it with the Christian church at Merriam. G. Abbott, C. V. Strickland and Copeland, committee.

A motion prevailed that the name of the Hivelies Corners C. C., or Smith's School house C. C., known by the last more recently, be now changed to the Christian church of Thorn Creek Township, Whitley Co., Ind., and be so recorded.

Report of committee on aggrievances in the case of the letters from the secretary of the North Manchester church; said report was rejected, and the case referred back to them for their further consideration, and a better report, as their report did not decide the case, only referred it back to N. M. to be tried by the executive board.

Adjourned to meet on tomorrow morning at 8 o'clock. Benediction by D. W. Jones.

THIRD DAY—MORNING SESSION.

Conference met per adjournment, at 8 o'clock. President in the chair. Singing as usual, led by Wm. Knappe. Scripture reading by Rev. Miller, of Goshen. Prayer by P. L. Wert, of

Waterford. Minutes of yesterday p. m. were read and stand approved.

A motion prevailed that license be granted to all ministers of good repute who labor in the bounds of this conference.

A motion prevailed that the name Union Chapel be stricken from the roll of conference, they having united with the Buena Vista Christian church.

Committee report. We your committee on aggrievance report the following: In refference to the charges against Bro. Ryker and Bro. Abbott we submit the following. We are glad to state that the following is the agreement of reconciliation. Brother G. Abbott and Brother P. L. Ryker agree to come on the floor of conference to give one another the hand of fellowship, and that all matters of the past be never brought up again or spoken of

Brother Abbott requests that he be reinstated to full fellowship of the church.

The delegates with Brother Ryker agree to use their influence to have this reconciliation brought about and Brother Abbott restored.

Also that the delegates and all the congregation join in giving the hand of fellowship to these brethren and do all in their power to keep peace in the church and conference.

In consideration of the above reconciliation, Brother W. D. Samuel agrees to become their pastor, and will move to North Manchester at once and take charge of the Christian church. C. V. Strickland, Thomas Whitman and Samuel Ohlwine, Com.

The report on aggrievances was adopted and we believe that all in the house gave the hand of fellowship.

Report on Christian Union.

We your committee appointed by Conference upon Christian Union submit the following report: 1st. What is Christian Union? It is not the unity of party, nor of opinion, nor of creed. Men may be united as the followers of Wesley, Luther, Calvin and Campbell,—as Methodist, Presbytirian, Baptist, Unitarians or Trinitarians, and thus be one in opinion, but this only illustrates the possibilities of confusion and division. This is only loving those that love us, while Christian Union is loving those that love Christ. Christian Union loves the good in all mankind.

Denominational Union is the division of the body, Church of Christ, (united.) Then as the human body is one, not from the sameness of its members, but being unlike each finds its completion in the rest, while all are fused by the pervading spirit of life. So Christian Union is organic and comes from the blending of living, growing, thoughtful persons who are led by the spirit of Christ Therefore

Resolved. That we continue to preach union upon the Bible. That we hold it as the grand old constitution, the principle, the standard, the directory, 'the all sufficient rule of faith and practice.

2d. That we will not exchange the name Christian for that of Baptist or any other name that would divide Christ's church. The name Christian is intended to bury all party names.

3d. It is but a due honor to Jesus Christ, the founder of Christianity, that all who profess his religion should wear his name.

4th. Let us take the admonition of Paul, and keep the unity of the spirit in the bond of peace. Was adopted. D. Hidy, R. L. Amber and B. Benner, Committee.

Report on Ordination.

We, your committee appointed upon Ordination, report the following: Brother Robert L. Amber comes to us properly recommended from the Paw Paw and Sidney churches for ordination. We your committee having examined him as to his fitness for the office, find him fully qualified, and therefore recommend that he be ordained, and that the ordination services take place on Sabbath morning in the grove before the hour of preaching. Committee, Elders James Atchison, Wm. Manville and Levi Marks. Owing to the rain which fell on Sabbath, the services were conducted in the church. Bro. Amber chose the ordaining committee. These were Elders James Atchison, George Abbott,

Thomas Whitman, W. D. Samuel and Peter Winebrenner. By these he was set apart more fully to the work of the ministry, and received his ordination papers.

It was moved by Samuel that the next session of conference be held with the Bluffton church. It was tabled; afterward a motion prevailed that it be taken up at 2 p. m.

By motion, the Xenia C. church was enrolled in the list of churches which will entertain conference.

Report on Sabbath School.

Whereas:—The Sabbath school provides ways for the development of talent, otherwise dormant, and opens up means for the cultivation of gifts that otherwise can scarcely bo utilized in the church; and feeling the necessity of reaching and holding the children of every community, and as this can be most easily done in the school, and by this means we can come face to face with those who can be drawn to our classes and thus labor more effectually for their conversion which is the chief object of all Christian work. Therefore

Resolved, That in every place where possible, (and only insurmountable difficulties may deter) whether there be preaching or even church organization or not, a Sabbath school be maintained.

That parents consider it their bounden duty to aid this work, by at least their presence and means, and that all pastors encourage each and all to become interested in the better development of this part of gospel work. Report was adopted. Jeannie M. Jones, G. W. Gloyd and D. A. McGinnis, committee.

Report on Conference Missionary.

We, your committee on the advisability of placing a man in the field to look after the interest of destitute churches, and building up churches in places where we have none, know of no other way or plan, than the resolution offered by Rev. J. J. Summerbell, and commend the spirit of which was, that the president or secretary visit destitute churches and look after their interests; and,

Whereas, there is no fund on hand by which a man may be

employed or paid for his labor; therefore

We do not think it advisable to place a man in the field until there be a fund for that purpose. Report was adopted. W. D. Samuel, W. Messimore and V. R. Miller.

Report on Advice to the Ministry.

We, your committee on advice to the ministry beg leave to submit the following recommendations:

1. To seek a nearness to God that shall be a protection against the temptations of the world.

2. To obey with the greatest care, the instructions to preachers, given by the Son of God and by the Apostle Paul.

3. To inculcate that which is revealed in the word of God, knowing that the Christians have one of their greatest protections against the encroachments of sectarianism in their faithfulness to God's truth.

4. We recommend our ministers faithfully to heed the admonition of the Conference, and of the Quadrennial Convention; not only in the matter of the quarterly collection, but in all other regards.

5. We recommend that our ministers preach during the year one sermon explaining and bringing before the people the commandments of scripture, with regard to prompt payments to the cause of God.

6. We recommend that our ministers accept and carry out the action of conference with reference to supplying destitute churches.

7. We recommend that our ministers seek out the church members that have ceased their activity and endeavor faithfully to restore them to their spiritual life. All of which was adopted. I. N. Compton, Alex Bayman and Levi Smith committee.

A resolution that the secretary visit and take the over sight of destitute churches, was tabled until this p. m., asking for the committee's report, at that time, appointed on this question.

Resolved, That we the delegates of the churches composing our part of this conference, vest in this body, the right to legislate for the best interests of the general church work in the conference;

that we pledge our power toward advocating and carrying out all the acts passed in this session, that tend to the advancement of the Christian church and cause of Christ. J. Amber mover. prevailed.

The Barber Monument case was brought up, and it was found that there was some $24 yet unpaid and due by a portion of the churches; but the delegates of delinquent churches responded with the $1.60 which had been levied upon each. A few dollars remained yet unpaid, but a few persons soon met the deficiency, and all was paid off. Brother D. B. Rollen paid the $5.00 which he had collected, and received his license.

Whereas, Some of our ministers of the Eel River Christian Conference have neglected to take up the 5 cent per quarter collection, and other work ordered by Conference. Therefore

Resolved, That we as ministers of the Eel River Conference or ministers of other conferences laboring in the bounds of this conference, pledge ourselves to take up the collections required by the quadrennial and by this conference. And failing to do our duty, that we be reprimanded by the president in open conference. Prevailed. Moved by Samuel.

Adjourned until 1:30 p. m. Singing led by Wm. Knappe. Benediction by W. D. Samuel.

THIRD DAY—AFTERNOON SESSION.

Met persuant to adjournment, at 1:30 o'clock. Singing as usual. Prayer by J. J. Copeland. President in the chair, who invited the two ministers uniting with us during this session, and the delegates of the two churches also uniting, to a front seat. While the audience united in singing, all came forward and gave them the right hand of fellowship, receiving them as co-laborers with us in God's cause.

Minutes of the forenoon session were read, and stand approved.

The motion on where shall the next annual session of conference be held, was taken from the table. The Conference then voted that the next annual session of the Eel River Christian Conference be held with the Christian church in Bluffton, Wells county, Indiana.

Advice to the Laity.

We your committee on advice to the laity, report as follows: First of all, let us remember that we are the servants of God, and should be ready at all times to do his revealed will; and that our success always depends upon united and harmonious efforts upon our part. Christians should ever walk worthy of the vocation where unto they are called, ever to be loving, kind and forbearing one toward another, bearing each other's burdens, (and so fulfill the law of Christ,) uniting heartily with your pastor in every good word and work; ever be engaged in the Master's cause. Do your part well; pay your pastor; fulfill all your obligations; see to it that the contract with your pastor is fulfilled. Be punctual in attending all the services of the church; be at and help sustain the prayer meeting; take up your cross; aid the Sabbath school work; do all you can for the Master and walk humbly before God. Adopted. J. Atchison, L. Marks and V. R. Miller, Committee.

A resolution prevailed, that the lengthy printed paper presented by J. J. Summerbell, be so changed that "president or" be stricken out, where in several places it reads president or secretary, and make it read secretary, only, and where blank sum occours, make it read $20. The paper refers to many things—is a Quadrennial paper, and is recorded with other resolutions presented by J. J. Summerbell, all excepting the whereases, these I omitted. *Sec'y.*

Report of Committee on Pastorates.

We your committee on the advisability of establishing pastorates submit the following report: The inconsistency, to say nothing of the inconvenience and loss of labor and money by the pastor living away from his or her charge need scarcely be mentioned, and has been abundantly shown in the work of the past.

The need of the church having their pastor in their midst is equally apparent.

The advisability of having at least one weak church connected with one or more of the strong churches under the care of one minister, or pastor, is also evident to us Therefore

Resolved, That this conference take the necessary steps to form the churches, which constitute this conference, into pastorates, and that a committee of five be appointed whose duty shall be to take charge of the work, and prosecute it to a successful accomplishment.

Resolved, That there be a called session of the standing committee, about three months before the convening of the next annual session of conference, for the purpose of confirming and establishing the work of said committee. Adopted. G. Abbott, W. D. Samuel and J. J. Copeland, com.

Report on Publications.

We your committee on publications offer the following report: Since the elaborate report of last year there does not seem to be much to add, except to make some corrections with regard to the statement that sufficient funds had been secured to liquidate the indebtedness on the Publishing House, and state some facts with regard thereto, and make some suggestions.

It appears now from some hints in the Herald, and other sources, that a considerable portion of that subscription is not available for use in the reduction of this indebtedness, and that some six or seven thousand dollars, or an indefinite amount, still remains unpaid; and some portions of this sum, if not all, is yet to be provided for. The Publishing House is not yet out of debt.

The Herald of Gospel Liberty in the mean while is doing pretty well. It has a circulation of about six thousand copies weekly, which will realize to the House $8,000, probably. This and the advertising patronage of about $1,000, making in all $9,200, as an income from the Herald alone. As to the S. S. publications and job work we are unable to give any definite idea of the income from these, but they are undoubtedly self-sustaining, and we think something more. Of the sum named above, about $4,000 is paid out as salaries to the editors and agent and clerk, and for traveling expenses of the editor-in-chief, leaving some $5,000 for the current expenses of the printing department, which we think only sufficient for the paper, and will leave very little to apply on the indebtedness of the House.

Although there has been some increase in the Herald subscription list, as also in the interest of the paper, yet the present number is far short of a creditable or even adqquate support of our only religious organ. It would appear that but about six persons out of every hundred of the membership of the entire Christian church of the U. S. and Canada, take the Herald, while, perhaps, four times that number read it.

The price of the Herald, which is still $2.00 to single subscribers, in this day of cheap literature, may be, and probably is, the chief reason why many who would read a religious paper, do not take it. There is one thing that may be said of us, that we do not support our periodicals as generally as we should.

The excellency of our S. S. literature is conceded by all, yet there is not that unanimity in its use in our schools that we could desire. The inculcation of correct scriptural doctrines and ideas in the young mind, seems, with some, to be of less importance or consideration than cheapness. Yet we are gratified to see the statement in a recent number of the Herald, that the House had reclaimed one hundred Sabbath schools to the support and use of our S. S. publications, which had previously used the Cook publications. This is probably through the influence of Elder Watson.

In conclusion, we would again urgently press upon our people the propriety and even necessity of giving a more generous support to our religious literature, as a means of greatly advancing the cause of Christ among the masses.

We would again renew the suggestion of the committee on publications of last year,—that of the much needed auxiliary of a tract society to our publishing department, to inaugurate and supervise the publication of suitable tracts for general distribution.

Resolved, That we, the Eel River Christian Conference as a body have entire confidence in the ability and Christian integrity of the editors and agent of the Herald of Gospel Liberty and

Sabbath school publications of our own Publishing House, and that we will give them our patronage and sympathy. Committee, D. W. Jones and D. Hidy.

A quilt from Goshen, with a good many names in it, was sold for $10.25—auctioneered off by J. J. Copeland. It was bid off by J. J. Summerbell, who afterward sold it to Sarah J. Winebrenner.

Adjourned to meet on tomorrow morning at 8 o'clock. Singing as usual. Benediction by Wm. Perdue.

FOURTH DAY—MORNING SESSION.

Conference met persuent to adjournment, at 8 o'clock. President in the chair. Singing led by Strickland. Scriptural reading by Samuel. Prayer by Abbott. Minutes of yesterday p. m. read and stand approved.

Report of Secretary.

I wrote out the conference minutes, and had one thousand copies printed in pamphlet form, and distributed them to the several churches composing the Eel River Conference. Also recorded the minutes in the conference book, making two full writings, and paid out some $2.00 postage, serving the conference. P. Winebrenner, Secretary.

Report of Treasurer

Of the Board of Trustees for 1887.

Reported on settlement 1886.................................$624.68
Error of last year's report............................... 48.54

Total for 1886.................................$673.22
Received since missionary fund................................. 8.50

Total.................................$681 72
Paid James Atchison............................$ 25.00

Total report for 1887............................. ....$656.72
Total missionary fund in the above..................$ 43.46

Belonging to Wabash fund.................................... ... .$613 26
W. Messimore Treasurer, L. W. Pullin President, J. W. Winesburg Secretary. Report adopted.

A motion prevailed, that it is the sense of this conference that the phrase "no more money" relates to the amendment on page 28. conference minutes of 1886, and applies to future donations and not to the past, hence does not effect the claims of the North Manchester Christian church.

Election of Trustees.

Election of trustees by ballot: Samuel Ohlwine, A. T. Studebaker and George McConnel, were all duly elected trustees for the term of three years, and so declared by the president.

For President, J. W. Sellers; Vice President, W. Messimore; Treasurer, J. P. Kitt; Secretary, P. Winebrenner; Assistant Secretary, J. P. Kitt; were all duly elected. The last four persons were elected for the term of one year, severally.

The Executive committee was elected by motion. A motion prevailed that all of the executive board or committee of last year be re-elected, which are as follows: J. W. Sellers, President, W. Messimore, Vice President, James Atchison, D. Hidy, C. V. Strickland, and P. Winebrenner, Secretary.

Report of Committee on Finance.

We your committee, appointed last year to report at the present session, a financial system for the use of the Eel River Conference in its local workings, present the following:

1st. We concur in the plan given to us by the Quadrennial Convention—in the general denominational work, and that we favor united and concentrated action.

There are local demands and interests that we can subserve by a conference system that will meet our wants, and to which we urge every member to give their hearty support.

2d. We advise that we raise a sinking fund; to be held as a permanent fund, to which we can receive donations and bequests at any time, and for all time to come.

3d. All money in the treasury of the corporation, from sales of property, and all money received from sales of property belonging to the corporation, in the future to be added to this sinking fund. Said money to be held in trust, by the trustees of the corporation, and to be loaned out at legal rate of interest, and the interest only to be used as conference directs, trustees concurring therein.

4th. We also recommend that the interest above specified be used for the best interests of the cause in the bounds of the conference during the year, and none of the interest so accruing shall be transfered to the principal of the sinking fund.

5th. We also recommend to the conference the advisability of assessing each member of the different churches belonging to this conference, the sum of ten cents per quarter, to be paid to the pastor or clerk, quarterly, as a fund for use in conference, and the pastor and clerk shall use their best endeavors to collect this assessment, and pay the same over to the treasurer of the conference, taking his receipt for the same. Adopted. Committee. A. M. Simpson, C. Myers, Alex Bayman J. W. Winesburg and John Phillips.

A motion offered by Simpson. prevailed, that we appoint the officers—the executive committee and the trustees the legal agents to receive notes, bequests, or any donation. to the sinking fund; and that the same be handed to the treasurer of corporation, and a receipt given for the same.

Report of committee on Leesburg: We visited the church and found it prospering. Adopted. J. Atchison and Wm. Manville. committee.

A motion prevailed that each church may appoint one or more persons to collect the ten cents per quarter, per member. as required in the report of committee on finance.

Report on Temperance.

Whereas. It is proved beyond all doubt that nine tenths of all the sorrow, suffering, crime and useless expenditure of money is due directly or indirectly to the use of intoxicants. Therefore

Resolved, That we make use of every means in our power to prevent the use of intoxicants in every form. And as we believe. tobacco has a similarly, though not to the same extent, inguri ou effect upon the human system, Therefore

Resolved, That all our young people be admonished, that they defile not the temple of God by the use of this pernicious drug. Adopted. Committee, Jeannie M. Jones and George Whicker.

Report on Woman's Rights.

Whereas, We believe that every person is obligated to use and improve every gift of God, and to do all they can for the bettering of mankind; and

Whereas, Each person is accountable to God for the use made of talent, hence each person must be his or her own judge as to the manner of work, and as this is an age and land of freedom, not slavery, Therefore

Resolved. That women be considered capable of deciding as to matters of duty and expediency.

Resolved, That no judgment be passed upon the actions of women as such, but as individuals who are equally responsible with men to God.

Resolved, That the men of this conference grant to the women of this assembly the same liberty they claim for themselves. Adopted. Jeannie M. Jones, Eliza Robinson and P. L. Ryker, committee.

J. J. Summerbell moved that the secretary receive as compensation for his services as secretary the sum of $20. Prevailed.

Report of Committee on Education.

We your committee on education submit the following report: Inasmuch as we are living in an age of improvement, he who communicates should have his mind well stored with useful knowledge; and

Whereas, The mind without it is like the uncultivated soil, needing cultivation. But the mind impressed to unfold the claims of heaven, will give itself to reading and study. The world demands an educated ministry and the heart well seasoned with grace. Therefore

Resolved, That we as a conference, are friendly to education— that those who enter the ministry should feel the importance of its obligations.

Resolved, That we will with joy the omens of good growing out of our educational departments and appliances.

Resolved, That all ministers before ordination should be required to fully prepare themselves to fill the important office with dignity and honor.

Resolved, That we recommend our schools, namely, Stanfordville Biblical school, U. C. College, Antoch College and others, as our own, and urge that our people patronize them, by sending their children. And young men contemplating the ministry, we urge them either to take a course at the Biblical school, or the Biblical department of U. C. College. Adopted. Committee, Wm. S. Manville, Jeannie M. Jones and Wm. Perdue.

A motion prevailed that the minutes of conference be printed in pamphlet form.

By motion the Secretary was ordered to prepare for, and have fifteen hundred copias of the conference minutes published in pamphlet for gratutious distribution.

Treasurer's Report, August 20, 1887.

Amount reported at the close of last session, of all funds on hand..$ 97 08.
Sept. 21, 1886, received of J. Rittenhouse for Purviance...   1 50.
Total amount received last year................................. 98 58.

Amount Paid Out.

Aug. 15, 1886, to Messimore, Treasurer of the Board of Trustees,
Missionnry fund...$ 8.50.
Aug. 15, P. Winebrenner for State Conference......   5.00.
Aug. 15, P. Winebrenner for services per order... 10.00.
Aug. 15, Rev. Degeer.......................................   5.00.
Aug. 15, Rev. Culbertson.................................   5.00.
Aug. 15, Rev. Godley.......................................   5.00.
Aug. 15, Rev. Abbott.......................................   1.00.
Aug. 15, Doc. Shaffer......................................   2.00.
Oct. 12, 1886, to E. G. Thompson for printing
    minutes... 50.00.
Postage and express on minutes.......................   7.00.
July 29. 1887, for paper and pencils...................   90.
                                                         _____
Total amount paid out.......................................$ 99.40.
Over paid..   82.

Amount Received at this Session.

Missionary funds	$ 45.45.
Conference funds	71.03.
Over plus of collection	27.
	$116.75.
Deduct over paid	82.
Total amount on hand	$115.93.

Respectfully submitted, Aug. 20, 1887. J. P. Kitt, Treasurer.

A motion by Summerbell that the first $20 for expenses, voted the secretary, be taken out of the missionary fund, and $10 for services be taken out of the same fund. Tabled.

Later. A motion prevailed that the first $20 voted the secretary for expenses in visiting, writing for and to destitute churches be taken out of the missionary fund.

By motion the treasurer was ordered to pay out of the conference fund, the cost of publishing and distributing the conference minutes.

Report of Committee on Condolence.

During the past year death has entered the home of Elder J. Rittinhouse and taken from it the wife of his bosom.

The wife of the minister suffers days, weeks, months and years of weary waiting and watching, of lonliness and anxious care, while the husband is going up and down in the earth, seeking a bride for the Heavenly Bridegroom. As she is his co-partner in all his cares and trials, as well as the partner of his joys, it is fitting that when she exchanges the cross for the crown, we express our appreciation of her work and her toils, and our sympathy with the bereaved. Therefore

Resolved, That we bow sorrowfully to our affliction, and extend to the bereaved our heartfelt sympathy, praying that He who came to bind up broken hearts may comfort and sustain our bereaved brother. Adopted. Committee P. L. Ryker and D. Hidy.

Adjourned to meet at 1:30 o'clock. Music by J. J. Summerbell, singing led by Wm. Knappe. Benediction by Jeannie M. Jones.

FOURTH DAY—AFTERNOON SESSION.

Met persuent to adjournment at 1:30. Singing led by Wm. Knappe. Prayer by P. L. Ryker. Minutes of forenoon read and approved.

Report of Committee on Finance.

In view of the report given to us by the standing finance committee, we your committee would report that we concur most heartily in their report, and have nothing farther to offer, only that at some suitable time there be a collection taken to pay the balance due on the note given for the Barber Monument. C. V. Strickland, Committee.

Resolved, That this body endorse the action taken by the Quadrennial committee, effecting the union with the Christian Union. J. W. Bolton, mover.

The above was tabled. Later. A motion prevailed to take it from the table, when it was substituted by the following:

Resolved. That we rejoice at the efforts made for union of the Christians, and Christian Union, but deprecate the use of words "absolute independence," recognizing the duty of Christians to "bear one another's burdens."

Committee appointed on Pastorating.

The president appointed W. D. Samuel and P. Winebrenner. The house appointed D. Hidy, G. Abbott and J. W. Sellers, five in all.

It was moved that the motion to re-elect the executive committee be reconsidered. The motion was lost.

Resolved, That in the matter of elections of officers, candidates shall be nominated, and not placed on vote by motion and second, as the latter method is a barrier to fair election. P. L. Ryker mover. Prevailed.

A motion prevailed that the treasurer of this conference pay to the secretary the sum of $5.00, to be paid by him to the Indiana State Christian Conference, as a conference fund, per order of the State conference.

By motion, the president appointed delegates and their altern-